D1298599

The Horse on the Hill

A Story of Ancient India

by Jessica Gunderson

illustrated by Caroline Hu

PICTURE WINDOW BOOKS
Minneapolis, Minnesota

Editor: Julie Gassman
Designers: Tracy Davies and Hilary Wacholz
Art Director: Heather Kindseth
Managing Editor: Christianne Jones
The illustrations in this book were created with
brushed pen and ink.

Picture Window Books
151 Good Counsel Drive
P.O. Box 669
Mankato, MN 56002-0669
877-845-8392
www.picturewindowbooks.com

Printed in the United States of America.

Library of Congress Cataloging-in-Publication Data
Gunderson, Jessica.
The horse on the hill/by Jessica Gunderson; illustrated
by Caroline Hu.
p. cm. — (Read-it! chapter books. Historical tales)
Includes bibliographical references.
ISBN 978-1-4048-5222-8
1. India—History—To 324 b.c.—Juvenile fiction.
[1. India—History—To 324 b.c.—Fiction. 2. Horses—
Fiction.] I. Hu, Caroline, ill. II. Title.
PZ7.G963Ho 2009
[Fic]—dc22
                                2008032414

Table of Contents

Words to Know

ceremony: formal actions performed to mark an important event

chariots: a small vehicle pulled by a horse, used in ancient times in battles

conquer: to defeat and take control of an enemy

glinted: sparkled or flashed

grumbled: complained in a grouchy way

javelin: a light, metal spear that is thrown

sacrificed: to give up something for an important reason

shrank: drew or moved back in fright

surrender: to give up

whinnied: made a low gentle neighing noise (usually done by a horse)

Pronunciations

Atul: ah-TOOL

Brahman: BRAH-muhn

Himalayas: him-eh-LAY-ehz

Hydaspes: heye-DAHS-peez

Macedonia: mah-se-DOH-nee-uh

Malayketu: may-lay-KEE-too

Pauravaa: POR-ah-vah

Porus: POR-uhs

Rishi: REE-shee

Sundar: soon-DAR

CHAPTER One

The Warning

India, 326 B.C.

When I saw the horse, I knew we were in trouble.

The horse stood at the top of the hill like a statue. He looked down at our village.

My father, the king of our region, stepped into the palace courtyard. He stared up at the horse.

"He has come," my father announced. "And King Porus's army will follow."

Everyone in our kingdom knew what the horse's arrival meant. Rulers sometimes sent horses to other kingdoms. The horse's arrival was an announcement of bad news. It meant they planned to conquer the kingdom.

The horse would travel until all regions had been taken over. When the wars were finished, the horse would return to his land. Then he would be sacrificed to the gods.

My father, King Sundar, had a choice. He could fight Porus's army, or he could surrender.

Our soldiers gathered around my
father. My mother, the queen, came out
of the palace and stood quietly next to
my father.

The horse walked toward us. Behind
him, soldiers followed. They moved
slowly downhill like a river.

Their weapons glinted like water in
the sun. Some rode in chariots. Others
marched on foot.

I gazed at our shabby army. Our
soldiers were skinny and weak.
We had no chariots. My father stood
proudly, but his royal robes were tattered.

The horse drew nearer. He stood tall and proud on the rocks. His black coat shone, and his silver mane flapped in the wind.

I couldn't take my eyes off him. He reminded me of a horse I had long ago named Atul. I'd raised Atul since he was a colt. We spent every day together, and he was my best friend.

But one winter night a band of thieves came from the north. I had been feeding Atul in his stall. Hidden, I quietly watched as they rounded up our horses one by one.

When they came for Atul, I hid in the corner of the stall. I'd been too frightened to stop them from stealing my horse.

My father shook his head as though he, too, were remembering Atul. These new soldiers would take more away from our kingdom.

"We have loyal soldiers, but they are too weak to fight," he said.

I blinked back tears. We would surrender our palace, though it was crumbling. We would surrender our fields, though they were dry and barren. My father would no longer be king. And I would no longer be prince.

"No, Father!" I cried. I put my hand on his arm.

He brushed me away like I was a fly. "Find your sword, Rishi. If we fight, you will join us."

I gulped. I didn't want to surrender, but I didn't want to fight either. If we surrendered, King Porus would welcome us to the kingdom of Pauravaa. He was a kind king. He would feed us.

"Maybe we should surrender," I whispered, trembling. "I am too young to fight."

My father spat at my ankles. "Then you are a coward. You are not fit to be a prince."

As the horse and his army entered the village, our soldiers moved forward. I ducked behind them. I shivered from my toes to the tips of my hair. I was afraid, and I was ashamed.

The two armies faced each other. My father stood at the front of our soldiers.

The horse lowered his head as if bowing to my father.

Then the horse looked at me. His eyes were kind, proud, and full of courage. Everything I wanted to be. But I did not feel proud. And I had no courage.

A tall boy stepped forward. "I am Prince Malayketu, son of King Porus. Put down your weapons and surrender. Or pick them up and fight." Malayketu laughed. "But you will not win!"

My father was silent.

Malayketu glared at him. "Well, what is your choice?"

We held our breaths, waiting for our king's answer.

Malayketu tapped his foot. "What will it be? Surrender or die?"

My father looked at his army. "We will not fight," he said. "We will become subjects of King Porus, ruler of Pauravaa."

Our soldiers grumbled, but I could tell they were relieved.

"Throw down your weapons!"
Malayketu shouted. "You will obey me
now."

Shields and swords rattled to the
ground. Malayketu picked up one of
our soldier's swords and touched its dull
blade. "Garbage!" he said and threw it to
the ground.

I couldn't take my eyes off of the horse. He looked proud, but also weary. Each time Malayketu turned to pat his neck, the horse turned away.

Does the horse know the message he brings? I wondered. Does he know that his arrival is feared by villages far and wide?

Most of all, I wondered if he knew that when he returned to his king, he would die.

By the sad slant of the horse's neck, I knew that he did.

"Gather your horses and your chariots," Malayketu told my father. "Your property is our property now."

My father looked ashamed. "We have no horses. We have no chariots."

Malayketu's mouth dropped. Then he snickered and reached to pat the horse's shoulder. The horse grunted and moved away.

"A waste of our time," Malayketu said. He gazed at our small army and then looked at my mother, the queen. "But your army will become Porus's army. And your queen will be his maid."

Anger burned in my face. I thought Porus was supposed to be kind. I didn't know he'd make us his slaves.

My mother smiled. "It is better to be a maid than to be dead!" she declared.

"Your horses will need food and water," said my father. He looked at the tall black horse. "Especially this one."

I shrank behind the soldiers. But my father looked right at me. He knew where I was hiding.

"Rishi! Take the horse to the river."

I stepped toward the horse. But as I did, I tripped and landed face-down on the ground. My mouth filled with dirt.

Porus's soldiers doubled over with snorts of laughter. I even heard our own soldiers chuckling. I buried my shamed face in the ground.

"Get up!" yelled Malayketu.

I felt a warm, wet nose against my cheek. I looked up into the brown eyes of the tall black horse. He nudged me again, his eyes sorry.

I stood and brushed myself off. I didn't look at my parents or at the soldiers. I looked only at the horse. "Follow me," I said.

CHAPTER Three

A New Kingdom

I led the horse to the river. When we reached the water's edge, he looked at me. "Drink," I told him. I put my face in the water and took a big gulp.

The horse did the same. Then he drew up his head and whinnied. It was as though he were laughing with joy.

"You are brave. As brave as any warrior," I said. "I will name you Warrior."

Warrior lifted a hoof and splashed me with water. I laughed and splashed him back.

Warrior pranced through the river. He looked back, waiting for me to follow him. I swam toward him. He knelt, and I got onto his back. We galloped together through the waves. It was as though we had known each other our whole lives.

I remembered my old horse Atul, and I felt a moment of sadness.

When we returned to the village, Malayketu and one of my father's soldiers were waiting. "You will guard the horse tonight, Prince Rishi," said the soldier.

Malayketu laughed. "You are no longer a prince," he said. "You are now a slave."

Warrior snorted angrily, as though he understood Malayketu's words.

That night, I slept in the pasture next to Warrior. His large chest moved with his deep, sleeping breaths. Soon he would no longer breathe. Soon he would be sacrificed to the gods.

My tears melted into Warrior's smooth black coat.

The morning sun was hot as we prepared to leave our village. My mother fanned herself with her peacock fan. "Which chariot shall I ride?" she asked.

Malayketu snatched the fan from her and threw it to the ground. "You will walk," he said.

"Do not treat us this way," said my father.

"You've been conquered," said Malayketu. "How do you wish to be treated?"

"As befits a king," my father said. Malayketu snorted.

For many days and nights, we journeyed to Pauravaa. We walked over the jagged foothills of the Himalayas. We crossed small rivers and streams. Finally, we reached the Hydaspes River. Across the river lay Pauravaa, Porus's kingdom.

King Porus came to greet us. He was the tallest man I had ever seen. His crown shone with pearls and gold. He glared down at us, and I shivered with fright.

"The horse chose your kingdom to conquer, King Sundar," Porus said to my father. "You were right to surrender. But I am sorry to take your kingdom from you."

My father sighed. "It is the way of kings," he said.

"Put them to work!" Malayketu said. "There is much to do before the horse sacrifice."

"First they will eat. Then they will sleep," King Porus said.

"They don't deserve rest!" Malayketu protested.

Porus glowered at him. "I am the king! They will do as I say!"

Malayketu hung his head, but I saw him glaring at me out of the corner of his eyes.

"Tomorrow night we will begin the horse sacrifice," King Porus said. "The horse has done well for us. He has conquered many lands."

I shivered. Beside me, Warrior pawed at the ground, his breath steaming from his nose.

I hoped tomorrow would never come.

CHAPTER Four

The Sacrifice

Of course, tomorrow did come. I was put to work preparing for the sacrifice ceremony. Malayketu watched me as I carried bricks to build the altar. "A fine prince you were," he said. "But a much finer slave."

I ignored him, though inside I burned with anger.

My back ached, and my throat was dry. I longed for water. I remembered how Warrior and I swam in the river many days ago.

Warrior would never swim again, and there was nothing I could do to stop it.

Before the ceremony that night, I snuck away to visit Warrior. I had to say goodbye, something I hadn't been able to do with Atul.

He was easy to spot in the pasture. He stood taller than the other horses. His silver mane glowed in the moonlight.

"Tonight you will go to the gods," I told him as he nibbled grass from my hands. "You will be a hero in the heavens."

Warrior's large nostrils flared. The muscles in his great shoulders tensed.

He reared on his hind legs. He was telling me he wasn't afraid, and that I shouldn't be afraid either.

"If only I had courage like you," I said.

The next day, there was a great feast of flat bread and fruit, but I couldn't eat.

And then it was time. We gathered near the altar. A fire had been built in the center of the altar.

Flames reached high to the heavens. The Brahman, the priest who would bless Warrior, waited.

Warrior was led toward the altar. He held his head high. His tail streamed behind him. Flames bounced in his eyes.

The Brahman touched Warrior's nose. "Oh great god, we give you this horse. For two years he has wandered.

He has conquered the lands he has roamed. He has brought King Porus greatness and wealth."

Malayketu stepped forward. He twirled a battle-ax in his hands. The blade shone in the firelight.

"We give this horse to the heavens," said the Brahman.

Malayketu raised the ax above his head.

I remembered my horse, Atul. I remembered how I might have stopped the thieves from taking Atul, if only I'd had more courage. I took a deep breath. "Stop!" I shouted.

Malayketu paused, glaring at me. King Porus raised his eyebrows.

"Take me instead," I said.

CHAPTER Five
A Great Invasion

King Porus frowned. The Brahman frowned. But Malayketu smiled with glee.

"A human sacrifice?" said Porus. "But that hasn't been done in ages."

"Exactly, Father!" agreed Malayketu. "And that is why it must be done!"

"But . . ." said Porus, his frown deepening.

"The gods will be pleased," Malayketu insisted. "And you know what happens when the gods are happy. The gods make us happy."

"But he is a prince," said Porus. He looked from me to Malayketu.

"He used to be a prince," corrected Malayketu.

King Porus nodded. "Take the boy," he told the Brahman. "He has shown great courage."

I realized it was true. I felt fear, but I was ready to face it.

Two soldiers grabbed my arms and led me toward the altar. "For you, Warrior," I whispered.

Malayketu's eyes narrowed as he looked down at me. He grinned evilly. "Maybe we should sacrifice them both," he said. "The boy and the horse."

"No!" I cried, but King Porus looked thoughtful. "Would that please the gods?" he asked the Brahman.

The Brahman nodded.

Malayketu raised his ax. The crowd was silent, except for my mother's sobs.

My heart thundered. Then I realized it wasn't my heart. It was the roar of horses' hooves.

"Now what?" muttered Malayketu.

A group of soldiers rode through the crowd. "King Porus!" one of them cried. "Alexander's army is heading for Pauravaa!"

I gasped. Alexander the Great!

For years we had heard stories about
Alexander and his fearless army from
Macedonia. Alexander had conquered
many lands and killed many people.
And now he was here, ready to conquer
Pauravaa.

"Stop the sacrifice!" Porus ordered.
"We must get ready to fight Alexander."

My father stepped forward. "My army will join your army," he said. "Together we will stop him from crossing the Hydaspes River."

Soldiers leaped to their horses. Others ran to gather the war elephants. In the shuffle, Warrior and I were forgotten.

I ran to Warrior's side. "Follow me. We'll run away!" I urged.

But Warrior wouldn't budge.

My father grabbed my shoulder. "Rishi, you showed courage tonight. Will you show it once more? Will you stay and fight Alexander?"

I should have felt fear. But I felt none.

"I will," I said. I stroked Warrior's neck. "We will."

The war elephants trumpeted as we marched toward the Hydaspes River.

A heavy rain fell. Horses strained to pull the chariots through the mud.

Warrior and I trudged along with the army. When we reached the river, I saw Alexander's army spread out on the opposite shore. My heart lurched. Thousands of soldiers faced us. We would be no match for them.

But we had something they didn't have. Elephants.

When Alexander's horses saw the elephants, they reared in fright. The elephants stomped toward the river, their trunks waving.

"Charge!" Porus yelled.

The battle began. A javelin whipped past my head. Warrior lunged out of the way. I clung to his back, firing my bow and arrow when I could.

Warrior was so quick that arrows couldn't catch me. I knew that if I hadn't been with Warrior, I might have been killed many times.

Even though we had elephants, Alexander's army was larger and stronger. Soon they advanced to the shore of the river.

Arrows flew as we tried to stop
Alexander. I saw King Porus's chariot
in the mud. "Go!" Porus cried, but the
horses couldn't move. The chariot was
stuck.

I turned Warrior toward Porus, ready
to help. Just as I did, Porus stood up and
waved his arms in anger at his horses.

Then an arrow hit him, and he fell.

CHAPTER Six
The Prince and the Warrior

"King Porus!" Warrior and I galloped toward him.

We reached him just as Malayketu did. I jumped from Warrior's back and knelt next to the king. "He's alive," I told Malayketu. "We must save him."

Malayketu trembled in fright.

We put King Porus on Warrior's back and led him away from the battle. I heard the splashes and hollers as Alexander's army crossed the Hydaspes.

"They've conquered us!" moaned Malayketu.

"Now you will no longer be a prince," I said.

I leaned over the wounded king. "Have they conquered us?" whispered the king.

"Yes, we have," said a voice above me. I turned and gazed up into the face of Alexander the Great. Malayketu yelped in fear and covered himself with his shield. I stood up.

"Are you a prince?" Alexander asked.

"Yes," I said. "And this is King Porus."

Alexander nudged Porus with his toe. "King Porus, we have defeated you.

Now, how do you wish to be treated?"

Porus sat up weakly. "As befits a king," he said.

Alexander laughed. "I like your answer. These lands belong to me now. But you shall remain a ruler here."

I couldn't believe my ears. I felt a little disappointed. I'd wanted Malayketu to become Alexander's slave!

Alexander sighed. "It has been a terrible day. A terrible battle! My horse was killed."

Warrior grunted and lowered his head.

"I need another horse," continued Alexander. "One who is brave. One who will carry me to battle."

Warrior let out a soft whinny. I stroked his nose. I knew what I must do.

"This horse is strong and brave. His name is Warrior," I told Alexander. I took a deep breath. "He is yours."

Alexander nodded. "Together, Warrior and I will conquer the world!"

Warrior nosed against my shoulder. He nodded as though pleased to be joining Alexander.

"You're a fine prince," Alexander said to me as he led Warrior away.

Warrior whinnied in agreement. Malayketu sobbed beneath his shield.

Alexander didn't conquer the world. He didn't even conquer India. He left our country one year later.

It is hard to believe, but after the battle Malayketu and I became friends. King Porus and my father became friends, too. Porus' rule over us was always fair.

Over the years, I often thought of
Warrior, and I was happy. I knew he was
happy, too. And maybe sometimes he
thought of me. After all, we'd saved each
other's lives. And that is something not
easily forgotten.

Afterword
The Sacrifice Ceremony

Ancient Indians believed in many gods. They believed that gods lived in water, wind, fire, and the sun.

Ancient Indians often made sacrifices to the gods. They believed that the sacrifices would bring them wealth and happiness.

Many things were given as sacrifices or gifts to the gods. People often gave gifts of bamboo shoots, rice, or other plants. Sometimes animals, such as cows or horses, were sacrificed in the gods' honor.

Sacrificial ceremonies had many details. The ceremonies often lasted for many days. Food and music were often part of the ceremony.

Priests, kings, and common people attended the ritual. Priests, or Brahmans, blessed the item or animal that was to be sacrificed.

The horse sacrifice was unique. Preparations began years before the ceremony. A horse was chosen to wander the land outside the kingdom. An army of soldiers, including the prince, followed the horse wherever it roamed. The land the horse walked through was considered conquered by the king. Sometimes battles broke out between the soldiers and the people of the conquered land.

When the horse returned to the kingdom, the sacrifice took place. The ceremony was popular and attended by many people. The horse sacrifice was so important that gold coins were often minted in its honor. On the coin was the image of the horse.

In later times, Indians stopped sacrificing animals. However, they still held rituals in which a knife was passed over a cow. They did this to remember the sacrificial tradition.

On the Web

FactHound offers a safe, fun way to find Web sites related to topics in this book. All of the sites on FactHound have been researched by our staff.

1. Visit *www.facthound.com*
2. Type in this special code: 1404852220
3. Click on the FETCH IT button.

Your trusty FactHound will fetch the best sites for you!

Look for more *Read-It!* Reader Chapter Books: Historical Tales: